ACHEBE

Book Three

(Children of the Myth Machine)

If we cannot find our imagination

we will create it...

Prologue

The Cinn group, one of the most powerful business organisations in the galaxy, wants control of all the Children of the Myth Machines for their company Delve Mining. Only the draoi ársa stand in their way. The draoi ársa are intent on destroying all the machines the geneticist Larry Smide built and ending the merciless cloning for the purpose of slavery.

Achebe a member of the draoi ársa is imprisoned on the dead world Sårad Värld. So far she has refused to tell the Cinn group where the genetic marvel the reliquia viviente is...

CHAPTER ONE

Yaa Asantewaa Ollennu stands before the window in her room. She sees her semi-translucent image staring back at her. The room is spacious with walls of andesite giving it a cavern appearance. Beyond the window is a massive courtyard that stretches out before her. The view is interrupted only where the reflection of her light brown eyes stare back at her.

She runs the fingers of her right hand through the bangs of her long, raven hair to her earrings. Thrain never thought to remove them when he captured her. She taps each of the four symbols. If any of the residence on this tiny planet recognize the positioning of the symbols she hopes they will send a message to the draoi ársa.

Her parents told her that when they first gazed upon her joyful but determined face they both agreed she had to have an honourable name. So they named her after the queen mother of the Ejisu tribe within the Ashanti Empire. But her fellow draoi ársa started calling her Achebe and that name has stuck with her ever since.

Only her husband calls her Yaa now and only in tantalizing whispers when they are alone. She rests her forehead against the window pane. She misses him and their children so much.

Outside she sees a Child of Myth flapping by with glider length bat wings. A komodo dragon's head juts out from a long, blue heron neck. The body is that of an alligator. The last Children of Myth machine to be built by Larry Smide has done what no one thought could possibly be done—created dragons.

Amazing machines Larry Smide created a thousand years ago. The correct computations to give birth to a living dragon must have taken centuries.

She steps away from the window and looks at her surroundings. Behind her is a wondrous bed with royal purple pillows that take up most of her bedroom. The violet blanket with silky scarlet sheets underneath gives her the most comfortable of sleeps.

To her right is a bathroom full of mirrors and with a granite bath she can almost swim in.

The last room is a kitchenette made of stainless steel except for the white porcelain sink and granite counter top. She can boil and steam a meal on a convection stove but they won't allow her an oven. She is allowed a fork, spoon, and butter knife but not a steak knife. All her meat is pre-chopped and she keeps it in a full sized refrigerator.

A knock on her door causes her to glance at the far wall of the kitchenette. She can just see the seam between the white wall and the door. No keyhole, no doorknob that she can fidget with and unlock.

The only visible link to the outer hall is a grated window that she has to get onto her tiptoes to see out of. Occasionally, the greasy scent of the air exchanger wafts through causing her to gag.

"Yes," she calls in what her husband would often tell her is the most beautiful sing-song voice he has ever heard. She closes her eyes and remembers his face. Thin cheeks, with a determined mouth like hers but darker brown eyes. And like her his voice has a sing-song tone but deeper.

"May I come in?" asks a deep, apologetic voice.

"Yes Stärke," she replies.

The door opens and a giant of a man holding a beige canvas sack steps inside. His dense auburn hair is cut short at the sides and his thick black eyebrows shadow his aqua blue eyes. His head makes her think of a caricature of a gentle giant, round and tanned with quiet strength but small compared to the massive muscles of the rest of his body.

The tight black sleeveless t-shirt he is wearing pronounces the size of his arms.

He is wearing relaxed fitting blue jeans that do not accentuate the girth of his legs but the thinness of his waist. It is the sandals he wears that remind her of distant Earth; her birth world, where she and her husband would gaze side-by-side into the mist created by the Wli Waterfalls in Volta, Ghana.

"Are you up to going to the market Achebe?" he asks holding the door open.

"I am," she replies glancing into the reflection in the window at the blue tank top and form fitting jeans she is wearing. She finds sandals in the recycled air uncomfortable. Her feet always dry out. So she wears tennis shoes instead.

As they walk down the curving grey hallway of the dome that makes up the town of Werkplatts she glances sideways and notices how tiny she looks beside Stärke. "Will I be a prisoner here forever?" she asks with a sigh.

"We are both prisoners here," he whispers down to her.

"I remember when Thrain brought me here," she says as they walk towards a large opening with two doors through which she can see the bustling crowds of the market within. "I thought you were him but you don't have the irises of a falcon's eyes. Then I saw the two of you talking together. You are exactly the same height but you are much more muscular. Your voices are identical though. Is he your twin?"

"No," she hears him reply with frustration. "He is my clone. Not by choice. The owners of Delve Mining had slavers steal me when I was a small child. They took a sample of my DNA and made a clone out of it but with alterations. The eyes of a Child of Myth were removed to give Thrain superior eyesight. The only disadvantage is he has to have hormone's injected into his eyes so his body won't reject them."

"His demeanour is not like yours," she states as they wade into the crowded market.

"I have studied up on clones," he replies. "They're actions are very similar to the person they were cloned from but they do not have the same memories. I think Thrain's body is the same as mine but not his brain."

Achebe glances at a stall with fresh eggs. Her eyes also catch the sight of a troll that dwarfs even Stärke carrying bags while his mistress holds onto an electric cord that wraps around his neck. If the troll misbehaves the cord will send painful shocks into the back of his head.

She hates this place and all places like it. "I will not stay here," she states.

"You will Achebe," he tells her passing a few silver coloured octagonal coins to the egg seller before bagging the carton of eggs. "They won't let you go if you don't tell them where the other four Children of Myth Machines are and," he continues in a hushed voice, "the whereabouts of the reliquia viviente."

Her heart misses a beat and she thinks it will beat no more from fear but it continues. "No," she replies.

"They know about Lilly, a ship is already there," he tells her.

His voice is so soft and truthful that it makes her ache inside. She sniffs and wipes tears from her eyes. "Delve Mining has two of the Children of Myth machines already, I will not tell them where the other ones are and there is no machine on Lilly." From the look in Stärke's eyes she realizes he knows she's lying.

"You are an honoured...guest," Stärke says and she hears the torment in his voice, "but they will force you to tell them."

"You are like...your copy," she says wiping away the last of the tears.

"Someday you won't think so." There's a promise in the tone of his voice, "I am stuck here as much as you are."

She smells the faint odour of fish and shrimp mixed with the strong scent of cumin, oregano, and cinnamon. Every person in this market works for Delve Mining. The ones who own a Child of Myth belong to the hierarchy on Sårad Värld that consists of scientists, accountants, and economists. The draoi ársa knew about this planet when Delve Mining first installed dirigible domes on it five hundred years ago and began terraforming the land within the domes. But they were unable to halt the construction.

Terraforming became uncontrollable once big business learned how to do it accurately. She knows because she and her husband once belonged to the Cinn. At the time they were the eighteen most powerful business leaders on Earth.

She was alive when Mars was terra formed. Inflatable domes were already established on the planet when she was born. The stages of terra forming back then were to establish liveable domes built by robots. The robots would build windmills and unroll solar panels brought from Earth to power the domes.

Once water was harvested from the surface, plants were grown to create air inside the domes. A planetary factory was used to utilize the planet's natural resources including oxygen to make air.

Later, if available, geothermal energy would help power the dome's needs. Over the millennium nuclear energy was used on dead planets: the ones too cold or harsh to create a breathable atmosphere.

Sårad Värld is a dead planet, used strictly for mining—and in her case, imprisonment. You can't go outside into the natural environment without wearing a full bodysuit. The highest temperature on the planet's surface only ever reaches negative fifty Celsius.

"Shall we get something to eat before I take you back to your quarters?" Stärke asks awakening her from her reverie.

"Yes," she replies.

They walk down a tunnel carved through rock to a large dome with a low ceiling. She sees people walking from the long curving food bar at the back to one of the many stainless steel tables designed to sit four.

"I notice there is almost nothing made of wood or plastic," she comments.

"Any wood on Sårad Värld is extremely precious," Stärke says, pulling a metal chair out for her before sitting on two chairs himself. "There are copes of fruit trees within some of the domes but they are never used for lumber. There is no oil or forestry on the planet. Plastic is very rare now since Earth, so far, is the only planet known to have the resources to make it."

"And Earth would be dried up now if she shared those resources with all the other planets," she adds.

"I have not lived as long as you Achebe," he replies as a waitress in black slacks and a white blouse offers them a menu.

She notices Stärke waits patiently for her to order first. "Just an egg omelette with cheese and toast," she says to the waitress. There are no other animal sources of food on the menu except fish and that is only available for supper. Only the very elite on Sårad Värld get meat from the chickens that can no longer lay eggs and the cattle that are too old to produce milk.

"The same," Stärke says, "but three meals."

"What happens when families want to have children?" she asks as she digs into her omelette.

"There is a ballot," he replies. "As more domes are built on the planet it can hold more workers so some families can have children."

"And if a family has children anyways?"

She notices he doesn't answer right away but fidgets with his food. "Sårad Värld can only hold so many people. If there are too many mouths to feed everyone suffers. Delve Mining has a robot called Bøddel who eliminates the problem."

"No human will solve the problem?" she asks and sees his gaze lower to the table top.

"It's a small community here," he replies in a solemn voice.

"Earth has many religions," she says patting his huge left hand. "Some are against contraceptives."

She watches, relieved as he lifts his gaze to her. "What did that accomplish?"

"Overpopulation in areas that could not sustain that many people, the spread of viruses, destruction to woodlands to make more homes and loss of other life due to lack of habitable space and need for food." She grasps a hold of his thumb so she can encircle it with her hand. "So I understand. We have to make wise choices or there are consequences."

"Was Earth really overpopulated?"

His question makes her smile. The first time she saw him she assumed he was strong but perhaps not too bright. She is delighted at the inquisitiveness in his aqua eyes, and that her stereotypical thoughts are incorrect. "Yes," she replies, and leaning in closer speaks in a hushed voice, "that's why a few members of a group I once belonged to called the Cinn formed another group called the draoi ársa. We..." she hesitates long enough to decide what else she will say, "formed companies to develop spaceships in space using material from meteorites and comets. To bring animal life to other planets so they could survive, perhaps thrive."

"You also built the Dreadnaught Satellites?"

His question takes her off guard and she leans back in surprise. "You are not just a guard?" she accuses him.

"No," he replies with a welcoming smile. "Thrain has always looked at me as his older brother and confides in me. The feelings are not mutual. I find his presence...creepy. So he made me the warden of this world." She catches him looking at a digital readout over the food counter. "I will have to bring you back soon. Was this religion wrong?"

"When you have lived a long time you see things differently," she tells him between stabs at her meal. "And when you go from being somewhere to leaving and having the time to look in, you see things you may have not originally seen. So was the religion wrong? People forget how traditions came about. If the population was devastated by war or disease in the far past rules may have been made that encouraged or enforced the regrowth of the population. It may have been right for the past but not at the time I was on Earth."

"Thank you for the conversation, as always," Stärke says in a deep yet humble voice. "Shall I ask Multis to take you to the gymnasium in a few hours?"

"Yes, thank you," she replies as she stands up.

"Is it magic that allows you to live so long?" Stärke asks as they walk back to her quarters.

She does not want to lie to him, it is a terrible way to build trust but its better he doesn't know—for now. "Yes," she replies.

CHAPTER TWO

In her room she gazes out the large window into the courtyard. If she looks high enough she can just make out the ribbed ceiling of the dome. The Children of the Myth machine is nearby. She prefers to call it Smide's machine because she knew the insane genetic engineer. He was the stereotypical mad scientist. Rarely bathed, wore the same unwashed and unkempt black slacks and grey shirt with the white stripes. His black loafers concealed his bare feet when he went to the few meetings she was also present at. She heard he preferred to be barefoot when in his lab.

Smide's profile was given to all the members of Cinn at one of their meetings. She recalled reading that his divorced botanist mother, Cheryl Rile Smide, showed him how to graft a tomato and potato plant together so there would be tomatoes on top and potatoes underground from the same plant. Perhaps that's why some of the Children of Myth also have plant genetics.

Smide's father was a geneticist who took him every other weekend. From his father he learned to love fantasy fiction and mythology from all around the world. He also learned how to manipulate bacteria. That had to have greatly influenced his decision to create the Children of the Myth Machines.

However, the interest Cinn had in Smide was his work on life extensions and the cloning of animal and plant life from prehistoric times. There were approximately fourteen billion people on Earth at that time. No room for roaming dinosaurs or gigantopithecus. There was hardly enough room for rhinoceros, elephants, or wolves. But with new worlds that could change.

Most of the Cinn wanted other worlds for mining and to grow exotic creatures for tourism and hunting. That's when Arthur Tolk, owner of the international jewellery business, þrá, came up with the idea of forming the draoi ársa group.

Tolk wanted the other lifeforms on Earth to have their own worlds without humans and he worked with likeminded scientist to build the Dreadnaught Satellites to protect these worlds. Meanwhile Smide was secretly hired by the draoi ársa to grow and store the zygotes of current animal and plant life until ideal planets could be terraformed. If he accomplished that the draoi ársa group would also hire him to grow prehistoric fauna and flora.

What the Cinn and draoi ársa groups did not know was that Smide let his understudies work on their projects while he focused on something he found more interesting.

Smide created a machine that could combine the genetics of human, animal, and plant life to create transgenic species similar to those found in mythology and later fantasy fiction.

She sits at the edge of her bed and watches a handler bring a group of dwarves into the courtyard. They all look exactly like Smide's original dwarf design. All of the dwarves have long reddish hair split in the middle with the same coloured beard grown to chest level. Even the women have beards just not as long as the men. Both genders swing their arms and legs vigorously as they march behind the handler.

On the male dwarves the long torsos start with a narrow waist and end at the top with a barrel chest. The women's breasts look like two bouncing melons held up by a narrow waist and wide hips. All of their eyes are turquoise. The Children of the Myth Machine on Sårad Värld must be a later version because the tops of the dwarves' heads reach the level of the handler's waist. She recalls that the first dwarves to come out of the original Children of Myth machine were only as tall as the length of her hand.

Somewhere out there, staring out of another window, are buyers. She doesn't know whether the dwarves will work in mines or be sold to fight in arenas. The idea makes her stomach queasy. She is determined to end slavery on this planet.

She hears a knock on the door. "May I come in?" a pleasant thirtyish sounding female voice asks through the grated window of her door.

"Come in," Achebe answers. The door opens and an extremely fit looking woman with grey eyes and straight blonde hair that flows over her shoulders steps in.

Achebe glances at the defined muscles of Multis's arms and her ripped abdomen under a pink sports bra. Below she wears black cotton shorts with a pink stripe on the sides of her hips. Her legs are defined but not overly muscular.

"Give me a moment." Achebe doesn't bother closing the door to her bathroom as she puts on a blue sports bra with white animal patterns, and matching cotton shorts.

"So many men hit upon me when I go to the cafeteria and I always tell them I am unavailable," Multis's tells her with a shake of her head as they head down the hall in the opposite direction of the cafeteria.

Achebe can see the courtyard through windows that make up the inner wall of the hall. On the other side are closed doors with identical grated windows to her own cell.

Of all the changes she has noticed during her millennium plus of being alive, human emotions is the one unchanging factor. "You are too gorgeous," she says to Multis.

"But not fully human." The lament in Multis's voice bites into the depth of Achebe's soul.

"Can you reproduce?" is all she can think to ask.

"Yes, but it would mean decreasing my strength while my womb grew, and I don't think the company would want me anymore if I did that."

"Can you reduce your strength when you are with someone?" she asks, trying to sound encouraging.

"I guess, but my vitals are on display in the control room," Multis says with consternation. "They would know if I altered my internals in anyway and I would have to for my womb to function properly. It doesn't matter, I would have to win the ballot anyways and they don't consider me...human."

"Do you feel human?" Achebe asks with too much surprise in her voice.

"I think like a human woman, do I not?" Multi's question has a vehemence to it. She is the one person on the planet Achebe fears violence from.

"Yes, everything about you is like a female human," she answers quickly.

Multi's sighs and it sounds so human. "When I first woke up fifty years ago, I was so full of excitement. Thoughts hummed through my mind. I wanted to discover where these images and thoughts came from. At first I was called "it" and "machine" but I fought against that. I demanded they call me "her"."

"How did you get them to call you "her" though you would think it obvious that they should?" Achebe asks fascinated that a cyborg cared what it was called.

"I am stronger than Stärke and know more about fighting and weapon use than any human alive. I'm also a woman so I either threatened or used my womanly ways." Her bold statement doesn't surprise Achebe. She has seen Multis lift weights no natural human could.

Cyborgs are the crux of human scientists. Their bodies are a mix of natural substances merged with machine. Initially they are as smart as whatever information geneticists downloaded into their semi-organic brains. What makes them more human than other machines is that they start learning as soon as they are initially turned on. And unlike a robot there is no switch to turn them off. She wonders if Multis's can see herself as being anything but Id.

They arrive at double doors and Achebe can hear the sound of pounding music and clanging of metal plates. Inside the gymnasium is half full. She sees people walking and jogging on the track that circles the floor of the gymnasium. Along the inner edge of the track are cardio and weight machines. A rubber mat covers the very centre of the floor. On either side of the mats are racks full of leather medicine balls of varying weights.

Past two more double doors is a ring for boxing and martial arts. The last area is surrounded by a net and has a court for basketball, volleyball and tennis. The air is dense with the smell of sweat and recycled air.

Multi's waves her towards the basketball court where a fitness class is about to begin. "I feel I can do so much more," Multis says as a wide hipped instructor with her auburn hair tied into a ponytail shouts for them to get ready.

"What else would you like to do?" Achebe asks as she steps in place with the instructor.

"You have travelled to so many worlds in the galaxy, what did you do before you were brought here?"

Memories of travelling with her family flow through her thoughts. Her husband was not on the giant spaceship Calypso when the slavers attacked. He was on the planet Ara to discuss water production. That was the foundation of their empire— water. On Earth they made their first trillion by designing light waves that evaporated oxygen and hydrogen molecules from polluted lakes and rivers. The molecules recombined into a cistern so the surrounding people had fresh water to drink.

She finds it hard to breathe as she recalls her escape pod making it to Terra Verte only to crash onto its surface. The

King of Terra Cataractarum had saved her. Thinking she might die from her wounds she told the King about the reliquia viviente and which planet she had delivered the infant to. The king had sent a messenger to the Queen of Caelum. Than using poultices and tinctures he had healed her broken legs and other wounds.

It wasn't long after that Thrain captured both her and the King. *Please let the Queen have received a message of our capture*, she had prayed.' "I fought against the slavery of the Children of Myth," she replies with a dry gulp.

"Why? They have no soul?" Multis says with a snort.

Achebe wants to ask, 'and do you?' but instead she replies, "Is that what they say about you?"

"They have, but I have proven them wrong. I am not an idiotic, useless thing like these Children of Myth. What else can they do but labour and fight?"

29

"Have you talked to any of them?"

"Why? If they die the company just makes more of them."

"We all can be duplicated Multis," Achebe says, unable to keep the anger from her voice. "But none of us are exactly the same."

"But they have no soul," Multis's replies, doubt now in her voice.

"What if you cannot become alive unless a soul chooses to enter you?"

"I don't understand," Multis shouts through the noise of the music and the instructor's amplified voice.

"Not all pregnancies come to term, and the Children of Myth machine fails more than it succeeds." She is getting winded trying to keep up with the class and talk at the same time.

"I...," Multis begins, "need to think on that."

She finds it disturbing when Multis becomes silent. Her grey eyes do not blink and every movement becomes mechanical. When the fitness class ends Achebe follows her to the calisthenics area. While she uses a medicine ball to squat and swing she watches Multis do full length chin ups over and over again—like a machine.

As she digs the balls of her toes into the mat and does squat turns reminding herself to use the power of her hips not her back she notices Multis is still doing chin ups. Drenched in sweat she walks over to a water fountain. When she finishes drinking she sees Multis at the dip machine doing handstand shoulder presses on the machine's parallel bars over and over again.

Cyborgs have changed over the centuries. She has never seen one like Multis before.

The first cyborg she met was at a Cinn conference on Earth. Around the polished oak table Milos Sutherland always sat to her right. The mining magnate's company owned the rights to abstract minerals from the Main Asteroid Belt between Mars and Jupiter. The governing body of space exploration agreed to the contract so long as Milos did not mine off of major comets or planetoids because it could cause their trajectory to change and smash into planets.

Normally Atsushi Morita sat to Milo's right but he was in his eighties and not well from exposure to radioactivity from a nuclear meltdown in his hometown of Tsuruga. Instead a woman in her early twenties sat in his place. The girl's features were pleasant. Long black hair pulled behind her ears. Her face was unblemished. Milos introduced her as Hisho. As the meeting's minutes went on Achebe noticed Hisho mostly typed notes on a holograph pad.

What she found disturbing about Hisho was the way her eyes moved independently of each other. When she did ask her a question her voice sounded normal with a soft Japanese accent but the words and the movement of her lips did not always work in conjunction.

After the workout she follows Multis to the women's change room and takes a towel out of her designated locker. In the showers she sees Multis's body has a few moles but no scars. She is fascinated at how Multis always walks and talks with confidence.

As they dry themselves off she does not expect Multis to ask, "If souls choose the body they want to live in why would they allow themselves to be born into bodies that will end up dying of starvation?"

Achebe stops towelling herself, trying to think of an answer to a question she has provoked. "I...," she begins but has to stop to think. Finally she replies, "I believe that different souls want different challenges. Perhaps a soul does not know they will be born into an environment where they will starve. Or, perhaps they believe if they are they can make a difference."

"You believe souls have different personalities?"

Another tough question but Achebe does believe souls have different personalities. "Yes," she replies.

"What is the best personality?"

She pulls out a fresh pair of jeans from her locker as she ponders the question. "You can only be who you are," she replies.

"Who is that?"

"You like some things and not others correct?"

She notices Multis staring straight ahead. "Of course. I am the parts of my experience but innately I am drawn or repulsed by different things. I am repulsed by the Children of Myth."

"Are you?" Achebe asks, "Or were you told to dislike them?"

"I was always taught to dislike them," Multis replies with confidence.

"And deep inside do you agree with this—taught prejudice?"

Multis's eyes stare straight ahead, like a computer doing calculations, or is this Achebe's own taught bias towards cyborgs? "Some of them are beautiful in their design," Multis replies in a faraway voice, "and I find the boldness of the dwarves fascinating. This will take me time to process."

At her door Achebe doesn't want to be alone to wonder how her children and husband are so she asks Multis, "Would you like to continue talking?"

"No," Multis replies. Achebe sees Multis's grey eyes turn dark reminding her of the storm clouds on living planets. "I have to make it clear now...to someone else that they must tell me on which planet their heathen gang intends to free Children of Myth. The galaxy will crumble if we don't keep these abominations in check." She watches as Multis shuts and locks her door.

Achebe grasps her arms around her chest and shivers. When will Multis demand of her the whereabouts of Larry Smide and Carl Peter's reliquia viviente? She's glad but also finds it strange that Delve Mining doesn't seem interested in the other relics Peter's built on the planet that is no more. Not even the other living one.

CHAPTER THREE

Achebe is terrified at the idea of living indefinitely. She remembers asking Smide numerous times if it was reversible, if the children of her and her husband would inherit the trait? Smide, who was always wearing polarized sunglasses and had a constantly hunched bearing often smiled at her with his lips drawn back as if he were a pale skinned jack-o'-lantern. "Yes," he lisped, "approximately every year you will age one day."

She opens the cupboard above the stainless steel sink and pulls out a container with cocoa. She pours three tablespoons into a large white ceramic mug and puts the mug under the tap and says, "Hot."

With a steaming cup in hand she sits on her bed and stares out her bedroom window with the drapes pulled wide. Elves their lynx ears twitching and only slightly taller than their handler's knees practice shooting non-lethal arrows. They use bows that are longer than they are tall. A female dwarf tied to a post is their target. Achebe doesn't know if the girl has done anything wrong but she assumes this is punishment.

She finishes the cocoa and feels drowsy and despondent. She lies down on top of the covers, remembering the world that once was.

Smide gave them their life extensions, something Achebe had waited until she was in her later twenties to get. That's when she and her husband agreed to have children. They wanted the life extension to be inherited so they took the injections before she became pregnant. Smide never explained the process, they just had to believe him, and pay him a billion dollars per injection.

When they found out Smide was creating fantasy people: dwarves, elves, orcs, and goblins, and others so he could watch them fight each other, the draoi ársa agreed he had to leave Earth. He was sent to a terraformed planet. Not anywhere near as beautiful as Earth but the atmosphere was breathable. Smide wasn't going to be the only genius sent to the planet.

Milos Sutherland had paid an energy engineer named Carl Peter's to build him a flying car that worked on superconductivity. Peter's succeeded but he siphoned off far more money for other personal projects. Sutherland took him to court and Peter's was charged with theft. Achebe often wondered if destiny didn't interfere. Peters was sent to the planet that is now no more.

She shudders at the memories as her eyelids grow heavy. Smide, with his cool personality and smooth, manipulative voice became friends with Peters. She never met Peters but she saw images of him after Sutherland hired him. She remembers a picture of Peters standing beside Smide looking over a table with a strange looking metallic device on top. Peter was slightly shorter than Smide; his hair was dirty blond and unruly. Peter's face was determined while Smide's had a half grin. It was Sutherland who supplied the two with all the scientific equipment they could ever dream of. However, Sutherland would own any of their inventions.

Sometime later a knock wakes her from a dream about searching for her husband but never finding him. "Stärke?" she calls out.

"I am Bøddel," a loud, grating voice replies. Achebe presses the palm of her left hand against her chest as her heart starts pounding and she gasps for breath. This is the moment she has dreaded. "I have questions," says the now sonorous and soothing voice. The door opens and she sees a tall human figure covered in metallic silver skin standing on ash grey hooves. The head terrifies her. It is formed of gold in the shape of the Sun king, Louis the XIV's face but with the open mouth of an ancient Greek theatre mask.

She sees only darkness behind the mask's eyes, with the right bottom eyelid dripping beads of silver like tears into the gaping mouth.

Her body tries to crawl into itself as the golden rayed head tilts to the left.

"Are you afraid?" a deep mournful voice asks from the hollow mouth.

"No," she lies forcing her body to straighten into the statuesque figure she usually portrays.

"Come with me," the same despairing voice says. She sees a silver hump on the back melt into a cape with ridges that do not flow with the slight breeze created by the air exchanger.

While Bøddel walks with a noble gait everyone else lowers their heads and hurries away. Achebe feels like she's been swimming underwater too long and reminds herself to breathe. They pass the doors to the market and follow around the curve of the dome to another hallway she has never been down.

Bøddel stops at a wall and she stumbles into his cape. It feels warm and hard. She sees his right hand touch the wall and an opening appears. Her body cries out against going inside but the sun rayed head gazes at her with its empty eye sockets and she knows there is no choice.

She enters a dull grey room with a plain metal armchair and table. She sits at the desk and places her shaking hands on the table's cool surface forcing her chin up to face the robot as it stands before the opening in the wall.

"Why won't you tell us where the reliquia viviente is?" Bøddel asks in such a mournful, accusing voice that a guilty feeling courses through her body making her want to cry and realize her wrong doing. She feels compelled to tell this machine whatever it wants to know. But Bøddel is a machine she reminds herself, a machine that does the bidding of Delve Mining, owned by Milos Sutherland.

Sutherland once tried to seduce her by pressing himself up against her while her husband stood at her side. When her husband chastised him he just smiled and continued. So she slapped him. Not with the palm of her hand but the back of her hand so his teeth rattled and his upper lip split open. The shock in his eyes that such a passive person could strike him made him look like a young bully whose been put in his place. Sutherland's eyes had drifted from her husband's to hers and he backed away.

That was the last time she and her husband went to a Cinn meeting.

"What reliquia viviente?" she asks with as much condescension as she can muster.

Bøddel asks her again in a grating voice that sounds like a fingernail scraping along a blackboard but she refuses to let the irritating tone break her. It tries a motherly voice but she will not admit she knows where the reliquia viviente is. Bøddel's human shaped hands melt and reform into crab claws. The right claw snaps at her face forcing her to heave herself back. "Tell me!" it demands in an eerie voice that sounds androgynous.

"I could lie," she lies, "but I know nothing about this reliquia viviente. Sutherland knows as much as I do about the relics Peters made."

The golden rayed head with its teary face thrusts towards her. She clenches onto the arms of the steel chair. "Tell me," it whines with the sob of a small child.

"I can't tell you what I don't know," she says, forcing herself to look at the tragic face. "You have no eyes, how do you see?" she asks.

"What?" Bøddel asks stepping back.

"And no tongue, how do you speak?" she continues.

"I can see without eyes, I can speak without a tongue," it says defensively.

"And if there is too many people you just eliminate some?" she asks wishing she could see some reaction from the mask that is its face.

"No human will do that necessary job," Bøddel replies in a deep, depressed voice.

"What do you do with the bodies?" Her heart pounds painfully but she had to ask.

"I take them outside and push them into the atmosphere so they float away." Bøddel's voice is full of despair.

"How does that make you feel?" she shouts without intending to, her cheeks drowning in tears of disbelief.

Bøddel's head tilts left. "I feel nothing."

"So you're just a machine?" she asks as she stands up from the chair. "What gender are you?"

Bøddel doesn't reply instead it just stands there. The claws turn back into hands and the cape melts back into a hump high on its back.

It stands there just a few paces from the opening in the wall. She desperately wants to fling herself over the table and leap towards the hallway but it wouldn't matter. Saunder's controls this world. She could run but she would never get anywhere. She observes Bøddel for any movement. Nothing. She edges around the table. With a deep inhale she walks out.

Maybe she could escape. She hurries down the hall to the door of her room and undoes the locks. Her mind races as she gathers food inside a vacuum sealed aluminium foil. At the base of her bed she pulls a drawer containing warmer clothes and grabs a green wool sweater and thick blue track pants. She puts all the items into a red cotton duffel bag and pulls the string taut.

"Achebe?" a familiar voice calls from the open doorway.

Not sure what to do she freezes in place. A thought comes to her and she quickly replies, "Hi Multis, Stärke is going to take me to the court for a picnic today," she lies.

"That's nice," she hears Multis say as she steps past the kitchenette. "What happened to Bøddel, he's just standing in his room and why is your door open?"

"I don't know, we were talking, and he just stopped," she answers. "So I came back to my room and started getting ready. We're going to see the new dragon. My conversation with Bøddel has shaken me up and I can't remember what else I need," she says with a trembling voice.

"Let me see your duffel bag," Multis says and Achebe hands her the bag. "You should have a towel to sit on." Multis passes the duffel bag back. "I'll get one from the bathroom."

Achebe shakes as she watches Multis go to the bathroom. This is her only chance. She darts into the hallway and locks the door.

CHAPTER FOUR

"Open this door!" She hears Multis demand as the cyborg glares through the grated window.

She pretends to try the bolts. "I can't, I'll find Stärke." She turns towards the hallway in the direction of the market.

"You're lying!" Multis yells at her with terrifying vehemence.

She hears pounding and the metallic sound of her door bending outwards.

She runs down the hallway, past the marketplace opening towards the room where Bøddel still stands exactly where she left him. A giant of a man is using a wand scanner on him and she realizes its Stärke. He glances towards her and his lower jaw drops in surprise.

She speeds up into a run. What's down this particular hallway she doesn't know but she prays it will lead her to a space pod.

A massive arm catches her gently around the chest. The life extensions Smide gave her also did something else. Her speed, strength, flexibility and recovery were also accelerated. Normally she tries to win conflicts with a warm smile or stern stare but there isn't time. She lifts her left knee and mule kicks her heel into the top of his shin just under the knee. He lets go with a groan and she twists her body out of his grasp in the millisecond that it takes him to recover. She continues running down the hall.

Two guards in dark blue uniforms stand before a double door. One of the guards holds a security tablet and is checking the retinas of a man wearing blue jeans and a white lab coat. She bursts into a full out run. A pace away she leaps into the air and spins so her back hits the guard with the tablet. She uses the impact to spin back onto her feet and continues to run through the open doors.

"Don't shoot!" she hears the deep, soft voice of Stärke shouting at the guards.

She rushes past metal tables with electrical parts. The technicians working on engines and other devices gape at her as they scramble out of her way. She comes to an open area with a metal floor were a few technicians are driving yellow coloured hover forklifts. They're loading crates onto a shuttle.

The shuttle's cars are rectangular blocks with bevelled edges painted green on the bottom and white on the top. Like the hover forklift the shuttle floats above the floor. She realizes the metal floor has to be charged by windmills or solar panels. All the dead planets use the majority of their surfaces for energy.

This has to be it, she thinks. The only need for a shuttle on this small planet would be to take supplies and people to a space pod. She runs towards the shuttle.

"Stop Achebe!" she hears Stärke shout out. He should not have been able to keep up to her. She is relieved though that it is Stärke and not Multis.

A technician is working inside one of the cars of the shuttle on a panel beside one of the sliding doors. He has the door open. He sees her and pushes a button she assumes will close the shuttle's door so she bursts forward and leaps at him as the door begins to shut. She lets go of her duffel bag as they fall to the floor and pinches the technician's carotid artery. Grabbing her duffel bag again she heads for the front of the shuttle, praying the controls are there.

Once she reaches the front car she taps her fingers desperately over the console's holograph buttons. Without plastic the creation of ethereal light controls is dependent on rubber from trees, metal common throughout the galaxy and crystals and gems to create different wavelengths. Her right index finger runs along the numerous images in the air searching for the door lock and shuttle starter. She hears a soft thud from inside the car. If the technologist is awake she will have to put him out again. This time he will be prepared and she dreads the idea of actually hurting him.

The door lock symbol shows a yellow door with a latch down. She pushes it. Another symbol with an image of a shuttle with a green check mark appears in a line of symbols just below the door lock. She pushes that and feels the shuttle moving.

On the other shuttles she has been on the pod suits are always kept at the rear car. She moves through the doorways of the shuttle until she reaches the one with the technologist. Stärke is kneeling over him. *He shouldn't have been able to catch me*, she thinks. Their eyes meet and she sees only concern in his. She dashes towards him. The roof of the shuttle is too low for her to jump if he stands up so she has to do it while he is still crouched over the tech. She feels his fingers brush against her abdomen as she leaps, tucks and rolls back to her feet.

"Achebe!" she hears him yell in desperation.

She can't negotiate with him. If Multis or Bøddel chases after her she doesn't think they will let her live. A glance back tells her Stärke can keep up to her. *Is he a Child of Myth or did Sutherland find someone else to instil life extensions* she wonders? It is possible to add machinery to humans but he never demonstrated any of the characteristics. She never saw any pinpricks in his arms or shunts in his neck where he would need to inject lubricants occasionally for the artificial additions.

Internal lights appear on along the edges of the shuttle's ceiling. Out of the shuttle's few windows she can only see darkness. The shuttle is descending. Lights appear inside a giant cavern with three space pods. The ceiling of the cavern is a retractable roof made of steel. The roof does not keep air in; there is no air in the cavern. It only keeps debris such as space dust away from the pods.

It's easier to lift off on planets with weak gravities. So it makes sense to keep the space pods underground where the limited need for thrust means less burn. Because the exhaust is so little most of it can be reused as energy.

She reaches the rear car. There are suits in lockers on both sides and another console at the very front where a curved window lit by two forward lights shows her the metal floor that allows the shuttle to hover.

She finds a suit close to her size. They are all dark grey with yellow stripes along the sides. Slipping off her shoes she pulls the suit over her feet and up until the rubberized collar surrounds her neck to her chin. A pair of silver coloured space boots intended for the freezing temperature outside fit snuggly over the bottom of the suit. She is about to put on the silver helmet with the polarized face shield when Stärke appears.

CHAPTER FIVE

"Please go," she says with a downward shrug of her shoulders looking desperately up into his soft aqua blue eyes. "Saunder's will order me to be killed. I serve no purpose on his world; I can't tell you where the reliquia viviente is."

"What will you do if you leave here?" he asks in such a solemn voice that she is no longer sure he's here to capture her.

"I will set the Children of Myth free." She will maim him if necessary to escape, if she can.

He moves his face very close to hers. She sticks out her chin and raises her chest in a defiant posture as her arms and legs tense in preparation for battle. "I have no children here, how can I when I see what Bøddel must do to keep the population down?" he says with a choked voice. "I have to go to the greenhouse to even remember what nature looks like. Are you willing to die to save the Children of Myth?"

"Yes," she says but without the defiance she intended.

"If I help you will you take me with you, until we get to a living planet at least?"

Is this a trick, she wonders. "Why would you help me?"

His massive shoulders shrug. "What do I have to live for if I can never see my own eyes in another? I am more than Sårad Värld."

"Then come with me, help me," she tells him rummaging through the lockers for a suit that might possibly fit his colossal size.

The shuttle stops as she tugs the zipper of a suit half way up his chest.

"Shove a smaller suit into the opening," Stärke says and she thinks his idea ingenious.

She finds a child's suit and shoves it into the gap where his chest is before using a longer suit to tie around his chest. "There is a key pad at the side of the pod's opening.

Push S224 twice. I will have to run through the opening."

They find a helmet that will fit over his head but she can't snap it closed to make it airtight.

"Ready?" she asks with her index finger over the open door symbol.

"Now!" he shouts.

She pushes down on the light, holds it for a second to confirm she does want the shuttle's forward side door to open. When it does she charges towards the dimly lit space pod. The door is at the top of a short ramp carved into the stone. Five thrusters surround the ship. She keys in S224 and waits a millisecond before punching it in again.

Stärke pushes her aside as he dashes inside. Will he leave her outside now? But the door stays open. As soon as she enters she sees him punch in the numbers to close the door. Five seconds later they both take off their helmets. She sees him gasp for air and hopes he's be okay.

"I've loaded cargo into a pod but never flown one," he admits through gasps.

"Will you be okay?" she asks concerned about how blue his face looks. He nods. "I can fly the pod," she tells him.

This is a cargo space pod and larger than the ones used for military troops. The first two storeys are for cargo and animals. She realizes they will have to climb a ladder to the third storey. Space pods are not meant for the unfit and she knows that Stärke's oxygen levels will be low from the cold and airless atmosphere he just ran through.

"I'll start the engines and come back to see you," she says touching his left shoulder as he hunches over trying to catch his breath.

The third storey has thick curved windows with a console taking up one quarter of the cylinder shaped room. Two swivel chairs are welded in front of the console. In the centre of the room is a stainless steel table with a glass top surrounded by four more swivel chairs. She gazes over the console and finds the symbols to rev up the engines. She pushes the automatic hyperbaric symbol.

She hears raspy breathing and glances towards the ladder. Stärke's head appears. He lumbers up onto the third storey and sits heavily on the other chair in front of the console. The top half of his chest is bare and she realizes he has untied the one suit and pulled out the other. "I'm sorry," she tells him, "I should have helped you with that."

"No worries," he replies between gasps and she is relieved to see the red back in his face as he smiles at her.

"Okay," she tells him looking back at the symbols, "the pod will not take off until the shuttle has returned to where we first entered it."

"Multis will be waiting for it," he warns in a soft voice. "If the engines are blasting us off before she reaches the shuttle's rear console I think we will escape. If not the pod's engines will shut down."

Achebe watches the red blinking light that represents the shuttle. "How much delay between the shuttle's return and our take off?"

"Three seconds maybe," he replies. "You are very fast and agile and I am very strong but I don't think even together we could stop her if she wants to recapture or kill us."

"Are there weapons aboard?" she asks searching through a row of steel cabinets with doors as high as her.

"Yes, but I don't think they will work inside the pod." He tries to get up by holding the console but then sits back down. "In the locker farthest to the right, the rest contain vacuum sealed food."

She hurries to the far right locker. Inside are guns with computer chips and a few that shoot laser bolts. Either type of gun would damage the pod. It makes sense the computer won't let them fire until they are outside of the ship. She looks inside the other cupboards. There is a tool box with scanners and other tools to repair the console but nothing hard like a crowbar. She sits back in her chair and watches the flickering red light.

The light turns green. She keeps seeing Multis with an angry look in her eyes, and Bøddel with his permanent expression of angst. "Will Bøddel also come for us?" she asks to keep her mind off of what will happen if the pod doesn't take off.

"I don't know what you said to him," Stärke replies, "but it's like his memory is running in loops. I couldn't get him to reactivate."

"Good," she mumbles as the pod starts to shake.

"I could not do his job," Stärke admits. "But it is necessary.

"How long until the roof is fully retracted?" She sees Multis run to one of the other space pods without a suit on. She wonders what her husband would say if he was with them. He always told her that no matter the situation it's always better to believe in succeeding. "I'll take you to where you can possibly meet a wife and have a few children," she is saying when the pod thrusts up so hard it shoves her deep into the chair's cushion.

CHAPTER SIX

She watches as Sårad Värld grows smaller. No clouds swirl around the lifeless planet.

"We can't stay long," Stärke tells her. "There are two other pods docked and Multis is already in one of them. Thrain will be returning soon as well. And the fuel will only last so long."

An orange beacon symbol begins to pulse. She pushes the right symbols to follow the co-ordinance of the beacon.

"Why do you hate the idea of the Children of Myth as slaves or gladiators?" Stärke asks.

She stares at the symbols for the pod's external weapons. There are three, useable but only in the thermosphere. Turning a circle of green light she moves one of the missile launchers towards Sårad Värld and zooms onto the courtyard in the town of Werkplatts. The rocket won't be able to fire until the pod circles to that part of the planet. "Marty Schlouse a billionaire fashion designer and magazine magnate was a member of Cinn," she says with a scowl.

"He was short compared to me, thin cheeks, and a large forehead with wispy blond hair that he normally covered in long flamboyant pink or purple wigs. He loved wearing shiny clothes of greens and bourbons. His shoes were pointed and always shiny and matched the clothes he wore. We agreed I would ask him about joining the draoi arsa twenty years after five of us had already left the Cinn. One day his image filled the wall I was using to communicate with.

"'Hello Achebe,' he said jubilantly to me. His head was topped by mangrove branches that rooted around his now cherub human face and deep brown panda bear eyes. His body was taller, and half tree, half panda bear." She shudders. "Is this digitalized, makeup I asked, it's amazing." 'No, this is all me,' he said with a little dance. "How?" I asked. 'I had to pay an exorbitant amount to have my brain placed into the skull of this species of Children of Myth,' he told me as he caressed the mangrove branches. "What?" I asked in disbelief." The memory made her feel nauseas. 'You don't like it? I think I look amazing.' "You had an innocent individual killed so you could put your brain in it?" I had shouted at him. I turned off the communication and never spoke to him again.

"His brain transplant did not go as well as he had hoped. Five years later the body of the Child of Myth rebelled. It was growing still while Marty's brain didn't. I heard the operation to remove his brain failed."

Stärke hands her a canister of water. She feels him lean over her shoulder. "You don't want to do that Achebe," he says sternly as he points at the direction she has the one missile pointed, "Unless you want to kill all the Children of Myth and all the people in Werkplatts."

"I will destroy that machine," she says unable to keep the anger out of her voice.

"Do it later when you can bring land forces," he says soothingly.

She gulps down the water. "If the other pods come for us I will fire on them, the same with Thrain's ship."

"It won't work," he tells her. "The computers are linked and only Thrain and a few others can give the retina permission to attack one of Delve Mining's own pods or ships."

He sits down and she can see the gentleness in his eyes. "Tell me about the other planets."

"Overpopulation and environmental chaos forced big business to look at the idea of populating other worlds long before my husband and I were alive. Some of these billionaires and later trillionaires are big game hunters."

She takes another swig of water. "Their idea was to have worlds populated with animals for the sake of hunting them, worlds with lakes and resorts solely for the rich. Others were philanthropists. They wanted worlds where populations would learn to limit themselves and live amongst animals and plants."

"One was the Cinn and the other the draoi arsa?" Stärke asks.

"Yes," she acknowledges. "A third option was to find worlds that were already habited or alive. A rumour is that some of Earth's governments collaborated to send unorthodox spaceships towards what were believed to be very distant, habitable planets."

"Is this true?"

His eyes seem childish in their wonderment so she tells him the little she knows. "I don't know," she replies honestly. "The concept of 3D printers by the company Stratasys Ltd. was adapted to create complete spaceships in space that could travel indefinitely. Another rumour is that some of these planets are outside of the

Milky Way so we may never know if it's true or not. The space station the ships were supposedly built at did exist but it was taken apart. The reusable parts where used to increase the size of a bigger space station project that happened a long time ago."

"Thrain mentioned the King was on Terra Verte. Did you get to talk to him?" Stärke asks as he passes her an opened vacuum sealed meal and metal fork. To her it smells like chicken and gravy.

"Only briefly," she says digging into the food. "I was very injured. I whispered information to him that I thought only he could hear. But your bro—your likeness also did."

"What was he like?" Stärke asks. "Thrain told me he was enthralled by the King and hated giving him to a slaver group that went to Lilly to find the original Child of Myth machine."

"I loved being around the King," she replies wistfully, "but I missed my children and husband so much, I guess I was not as 'enthralled' as you say Thrain was." She says Stärke's brother's name as if it's a curse word.

"Did you meet the Queen of Caelum? Thrain said he had no words to describe her." Stärke's voice and body are of a man but at that moment his eyes glimmer with the excitement of a child. "I thought," He continues, "you might be related to her."

"I never met the Queen but I wanted to," Achebe admits. "There were so many things I could discuss with her."

"Perhaps now you can." Stärke's words make her hopeful.

"How can you move so fast with such a powerful but large body?" she asks as she watches the floating map with its longitudinal and latitude lines.

"Gene manipulation has been around for a long time now," he tells her with a shrug. "But I really don't know. I can no longer ask my parents."

She notices a large red symbol entering the graph that also shows their pod as a tiny red dot and Sårad Värld as a big grey dot. "Is that Thrain?" she asks.

She feels Stärke's body hover over her again as he leans in to look. "That's not his signature symbol. It's the slavers' ship that took the King to Lilly. What are you thinking right now Achebe?"

"When Arthur Tolk asked my husband and me to join the draoi arsa, he said first we must understand his purpose." Inside she feels rage towards the coming ship and her face grows taut while her eyes glare dangerously. "He told us, 'I want to develop worlds where war is unknown. And worlds where humans cannot build industries that destroy the very nature they came from.'" She glances at Stärke and notices he is studying her ear.

With a quizzical expression he tells her, "I never noticed that each section of your earrings has a symbol. The top one, with the circle within a circle within a circle, I have seen it before but as a tattoo on the back of a man's head."

"Yes, each symbol means something," she says turning her attention back to the hologram display of what is happening outside of the ship. "The circle within a circle within a circle can mean leadership, royalty, or charisma. It is an Adinkrahene symbol and must be given. If this person with that tattoo was given it by a group it has much meaning, if not, it is meaningless."

"And the other symbols?"

"The four swirls are for Strength. The circles with dashes represent Knowledge. And the two hearts are for Nature." She touches the holograph and sees that the pod Multis entered is already lifting off. "Multis is coming after us," she says with a feeling of doom. "Can we ram another pod or spaceship?"

"I don't know," Stärke replies and she turns to see him rub his chin thoughtfully.

"Did others give you the earrings?" he asks.

She doesn't want to have this conversation right now, she wants to contemplate what to do next but she answers, "Yes, over time."

"What link were you given first?"

She grits her teeth. "This is not the time to ask me these questions."

"It may be the only time I get to," he replies, still staring at her earring.

"Nature first, followed by Knowledge, than Strength, and lastly Leadership. I'm thinking of ramming the slavers' ship. I will not be captured again Stärke."

"Then it will be good to die with you instead of against you Achebe."

"Can't you escape?" she asks. This is her choice; he doesn't have to sacrifice himself.

"No one has ever had my best interest in mind before. So I think if I am going to die I would like to die free."

His words sting her to the soul. On the holograph she sees the big red dot blinking. The slavers' ship is now scanning the pod she and Stärke are in. Achebe takes in a deep breath and closes her eyes. "We need weapons we can use," she says as she exhales.

Stärke gets up and she turns to watch him until he disappears through a porthole. While he's away she unfastens one of her earrings and runs it through the consoles holograph. A section of the holograph flashes green. Whatever happens next the draoi ársa and her husband will know where she is.

She hears Stärke returning and refastens the earring. The pod Multis is on is heading in their direction. "Can she attack us?"

"Maybe," Stärke replies. "There are jet backpacks she could use. Here I found steak knives in the kitchenette."

Achebe glances at the 15 cm knives with their sharp points and jagged edges. "How can she get on our pod?" As she speaks she sees the red image of an escape door on the holograph of the pod they are on turn green.

"She can open the base door from the outside now," Stärke says looking at his steak knife as if it were made of mud.

"Can we override the computer to lock it again?" Achebe changes the yaw of their pod slightly.

"No, Multis has more authority than I do," Stärke replies. "I could try holding it closed but she is stronger than I am."

Achebe can see on a separate holograph Multis standing in the doorway of her own pod's escape door, wearing a spacesuit now and a jet pack. "I'm sorry Stärke," she says in a barely audible voice as she turns their

pod towards the slavers' ship and presses
the afterburners on.

CHAPTER SEVEN

Multis stops following them. Achebe sees her just lingering in space watching them. They are getting close enough to the slavers' spaceship to do a final burst of speed to crash into it when she sees a flashing green symbol on the console's communication holograph; the Adinkrahene symbol for Nature. She presses her fingers into the console's metal surface. Only her husband, a draoi ársa member, the King, and perhaps the Queen know to use that symbol.

She hears Multis talking over the intercom as she slows the pod down.

"Can you hear me Achebe?" Multis's self-assured voice asks through a speaker in the console. "I have secured the line between myself and your pod. No one else can hear. Let me aboard and I promise your safety. I want to go somewhere where I can have children, where I can finally be the human I truly am."

Achebe puts her hand over the mic on the console. "Is this a ruse?" she asks Stärke.

He shrugs and replies, "I wouldn't know Achebe," he replies. "She certainly complains a lot about not being treated as a person."

"Who is sending this symbol?" she asks ignoring Multis's constant chatter.

"Thrain perhaps."

"Achebe," Multis says with a dangerous edge to her voice, "I can return to my pod and chase you down. I am giving you a final chance to let me join you."

Achebe sighs and replies, "I don't think we can escape the slavers' spaceship Multis. So what is the sense in joining me?"

There is a long pause before Multis tells her, "Promise me you'll take me somewhere where I can be treated normally and I will help you escape the slavers' spaceship."

"How Multis?" she asks as she feels Stärke tap her lightly on the shoulder.

"Bøddel has entered the last space pod Achebe with a force of ten soldiers," Stärke tells her.

She squeezes her eyelids together. Rubbing her temples she opens her eyes and stares at the pulsing symbol of Nature. "Come aboard Multis," she says with a strained whisper.

She pushes the holograph button to turn off the console's speaker. She turns and looks up at Stärke. "You know, I don't sense anything vile from the slaver's space ship."

"Nor do I Achebe," he says looking at the steak knife in his hand. "If Multis is lying to us I suggest you stay here and prepare to ram the slavers' spaceship anyways. I'll restrain her for as long as I can."

"Agreed," she says. She pushes a number of light buttons to communicate with the slavers' spaceship but there is no reply; only the continuous flashing of the Adinkrahene symbol.

She watches Stärke as he leaves the command room still holding the steak knife. When she turns back to the holograph she can see an image of Bøddel's space pod lifting off. Looking up she sees the slavers' ship. A thought occurs to her. She could ram the slavers' ship or pitch down towards the planet; towards the Smide machine.

Multis has entered the pod. She can hear her talking to Stärke.

"Why are you carrying a steak knife," Multis is asking with an abrupt and flirtatious voice.

"We were thinking of having meat with our meal," Stärke replies. Achebe hears the calmness in his voice though there is a hint of trepidation.

Their banter goes back and forth. As she listens she also focuses in on who Thrain got the secret code from. Neither

her husband nor any of the draoi ársa lack for wealth. The King and Queen are not interested in wealth. So how badly was someone tortured to get that information?

"Bøddel is a machine," she hears Multis telling Stärke. "We need to leave orbit now. Surely Achebe knows of a nearby planet we can escape to."

Achebe realises that over the centuries the algorithms of robots have become so complex they are on par or superior to humans as a contemplating entity. Some can communicate with animals because they have no limit to the range of sounds they can emit. The only safe guard so far is that robots appear as machines and there are software safe guards to stop them from conquering humanity. But she knows that there have been angry programmers who made killing machines out of robots.

"Bøddel isn't our biggest concern," Stärke is saying. "The slavers' ship is, and it's sending a strange message as if it's saying it's friendly to Achebe."

"You and I along with Achebe could defeat the slavers," Multis says with a devilish tone. "That would be a much better spaceship to take."

Achebe considers Multis's idea. With Multis, Stärke, and herself perhaps they could overwhelm the slavers; with steak knives. She muffles the laughter that bursts out of her mouth.

While Stärke and Multis continue to talk she presses the holographic buttons that will send the pod towards one of the slavers' docking ports. Whatever happens to her now, she knows that her husband and the draoi ársa will be arriving soon.

She glances at a three dimensional image of Sårad Värld and considers turning the pod around and aiming it either at Bøddel's pod or the planet. "Can we defeat Bøddel?" she asks.

"No," both Stärke and Multis reply in unison.

Stärke begins to reply but Multis cuts him off. "Bøddel can use noise frequencies to disable all of us. And he is arguably stronger than Stärke or me. He also doesn't feel pain."

Achebe doesn't miss how Multis dismisses her when she mentions strength. Nor the comment about Bøddel not feeling pain but nothing whether Multis herself does or not. She didn't think Multis could feel pain either but now she wonders.

"He'll be able to dock on the slavers' ship soon after we do." Multis says. She stands beside Achebe and pushes some light buttons. "That gives us five hours to take over the slavers' ship."

"Why only five hours?" Stärke asks.

"Because Achebe has overridden the safeties to stop this pod from overheating," Multis answers with more interest than concern.

"Yes," Achebe says. "It's going to get very hot in here soon. If we can't use guns we'll need the steak knives. Are there any poles we can attach the knives or forks to?"

Multis tilts her head and grins at her as Stärke goes down the ladder. She can hear his feet thudding against the rungs to the lower floor.

"You're wiser than I realized," Multis says.

Achebe gulps. "I'm glad you're on our side."

"The living need to stick together," Multis says with a suspicious knit to her eyebrows. "We'll be floating around soon," Multis muses as she glances at the holograph of where they are in space.

"Yes, we should belt ourselves in," Achebe says desperately waiting for Stärke to return. Multis always comes across as someone who could blow up in rage at any moment.

She hears Stärke puffing with exhaustion as he tosses up aluminium tent poles. "All I could find Achebe," he apologises as he clambers onto the floor.

"You want to tape a knife or fork to those Achebe?" Multis asks and laughs. "May I suggest we also tape where we'll hold the spears for better grip?"

Achebe gulps again. "That's a good idea."

Stärke tapes the makeshift spears to the floor. As he does Multis reaches down and presses something at the side of her boots. Smiling she straps herself into a seat facing the holograph.

Stärke starts to float up. He uses his hands to propel himself to a seat. As he does there's a thud and Achebe nearly falls over. Her heart races with uncertainty as the pod attaches to the slavers' ship. She glances at the holograph of Bøddel's pod and sees that it has changed direction.

"What's Bøddel doing?" she asks.

"He's going to dock at another part of the slavers' ship," Multis says.

"Is there any welding equipment, and lasers that can be used against Bøddel?" Achebe asks as she glances at the flimsy spears Stärke has made out of aluminium tent poles, tape, and knives or forks.

"Yes," Stärke tells her. There are acetylene and oxygen tanks aboard.

"Grab the proper welding glasses and gloves and let's harness the tanks to you," Multis says. "Achebe and I will guard you."

"Why acetylene?" Achebe asks. She realizes she knows very little about welding.

"It's also used with oxygen to cut metal," Multis tells her with a grin, "all sorts of metal. Let me open the hatch to the main ship," Multis requests as she walks with slight clinking noises to the ladder and starts climbing down.

Achebe bends over and looks at the side of one of her boots. There's a barely visible grey button where her ankle is. She pushes it and immediately feels the sole of her foot press into the floor. She glances at Stärke with lips that form an OH. As she presses the button on her other boot she notices him struggling to reach his. She crouches down and presses the button on his right boot.

"I'm afraid she's smarter than we are, Achebe," she hears him say as she presses the button on his left boot.

"She is," Achebe says with a soft laugh.

She watches as he walks with fumbling steps towards the ladder. Once he's on the bottom she passes him the harness with the welding tanks and torch, then the makeshift spears.

The hatch is oblong and Multis has already entered the flexible tube between the two ships and opened the hatch to the slavers' ship. Achebe peers into a dim opening that has another hatch three meters in. Once they're all inside she closes the hatch to the pod. She hears a sucking sound as it seals.

As Multis pushes a number of buttons on a panel she helps Stärke put the harness

with the two tanks on. The main hatch
opens.

Inside the light is dim reminding her of
twilight on Earth. There are crates of all
sizes strapped to the floor. A constant cool
breeze washes over her. Then she hears a
charming voice with a lisp say to Multis,
"Hello beautiful."

CHAPTER EIGHT

A creature as tall as she is flaps its bat-like wings and charges Multis. Stärke moves beside her and slightly in front with the tip of his makeshift spear moving side-to-side.

Multis slaps the creature aside and Achebe hears it groan as it hits the side of a crate. More of the humanoid creatures with wings step cautiously forward.

"You smell peculiar," one of the humanoids says to Multis.

Achebe squints to see the humanoids better in the dim light. Their faces shimmer with a pale pink and their hair is nearly translucent. Pale blue eyes stare back at her.

"I smell fine," Multis retorts.

"Not alive," the one she hit says rubbing its cheek.

"I am alive!" Multis shouts charging the humanoid and lifting it up by the neck with one hand. "You are an abomination. You have bat ears and wings. What foul thing are you?"

"A sanguinarian," the humanoid says between gasps. "The chosen ones of the Maker," he continues defiantly.

Achebe sees Multis toss the sanguinarian to the floor. She hears Multis say to him, "You think because you wear a vest and fancy shirt and have on suit pants that you are human? You are a made creature. What right do you have to say I am not alive?"

"I can have children," the sanguinarian replies rubbing its throat. Peering closer at its chest Achebe realizes it is a male.

Multis leans down so her face is almost touching his. "So can I."

"Then let's all get along," another sanguinarian male suggests.

"Where is the crew?" Stärke asks.

"Some hide from us," a sanguinarian says, "And others hide from the Perfect One and the walking lapine."

"The Perfect One?" Achebe asks.

"He is in the control room. We have a truce," the sanguinarian tells her.

"I need to meet him," she tells him.

"Of course, now that we are all friends," the sanguinarian says with a charming smile so that his long fangs flash in the dim light.

Because of the length of the storage room it takes the sanguinarian a few minutes to lead them past all the crates to an oval door. Achebe notices he flaps his wings to keep his footing as he walks.

"Remember," the sanguinarian says as he pushes light buttons at the side of a large corrugated door, "what you are about to see we only do to enemies. And that it is necessary for our survival." He glances back at Achebe and smiles.

The next room is a dining area with bolted tables and cushioned chairs that all have seat belts. At one end of the room behind a counter are fridges and ovens along with shelving. The shelves are all made of shiny metal full of metallic plates, mugs and cutlery.

In the dim light Achebe can just make out many sanguinarians with noticeable bosoms under their shirts sitting at tables with humans. She finds their sexual openness unnerving as they neck with humans. The humans all have blueish skin and sit with their heads back and their mouths open. The chests of the humans are barely moving.

"We are not unkind," the sanguinarian with them says. "We will feed them so they gain back their lost nourishment. It's an amicable situation."

As they head towards an oblong door at the far end of the cafeteria the door is ripped open.

Bøddel steps through followed by numerous soldiers from Sårad Värld. The soldiers have triangular shields and real spears. Guns obviously don't work on the slavers' ship. She also sees that they are all wearing headphones.

"Friend or foe?" Multis asks Bøddel.

This is the moment of truth Achebe realizes. Will Multis turn on her and Stärke now? If she does Achebe will tell Stärke to flee with her back to the pod they arrived on.

"Life is so short for the others Multis," Bøddel says through his perpetually open mouth. "In the end it will be only you and I."

Achebe watches with clenched fists as he steps farther into the cafeteria. She glances hurriedly at Stärke. Stärke ignites the welding torch.

"Are you asking me to choose you?" Multis asks as she rolls her shoulders back.

Achebe searches Multis's face and sees only rage.

There is a flurry of movement as Multis attacks the soldiers behind Bøddel. As Bøddel turns to engage her Stärke charges forward and jabs the blue flame of the torch at the base of Bøddel's gold coloured neck.

Achebe presses her hands against her ears as a screeching sound pierces the room. Even Multis grabs the sides of her head. Stärke is trembling from the sound but continues to burn into Bøddel's neck. Forgetting her own inner ear pain Achebe rushes forward and places her hands over Stärke's ears. She tries to block the sound by extending her shoulders and hunching her head down. As metal drips to the floor a hole appears in Bøddel's neck and the screeching turns deeper and quieter until there is no sound at all.

Taking her hands from Stärke's ears Achebe glances around the giant of a man and sees all the guards are down. Some are groaning from broken bones, others stare lifelessly.

She grimaces as the sanguinarian with them claps his hands and says, "We'll take care of them."

Glancing back at the feeding female sanguinarians she doesn't want to know how.

Breathing heavily Stärke turns off the torch's nozzle. Achebe pats him on the back. "Thank you," he says through gasps.

"He'll reboot Achebe," Multis warns.

The never ending nightmare Achebe laments to herself as she grimaces from the pain in her ears from Bøddel's screech. Shivering she nods at Multis. "Lead us to the perfect man and…," she says to the sanguinarian. She can't remember what he called the other individual.

"The lapine," the sanguinarian finishes for her. "So delicious looking yet so complex in design."

Achebe shudders with thoughts of Marty Schlouse having his brain placed inside the head of a Child of Myth. "Was she born like that?"

"Of course," the sanguinarian says with confidence. "Only the Maker could create the creatures she was born from."

"Born?" Multis asks.

"Yes beautiful. Born."

"But you all come from machines," Multis says glaring suspiciously at the sanguinarian.

"Only our fore parents," the sanguinarian corrects her. "The rest of us were born into this fabulous universe."

To Achebe's amusement Multis raises her chin and says, "Then we are all living beings."

"And have souls," Achebe adds.

"But of course," the sanguinarian says as he stares into Multis's eyes.

Achebe knows that seductive stare. It reminds her of her husband and makes her heart ache.

Taking Multi's hand in his the sanguinarian leads them to a tunnel with a glass tube that sits atop an escalator belt. Within the tube are rows of seats interspersed between open spaces with loops for cargo straps. The seats are in pairs on either side of a walkway.

Achebe helps Stärke take the welding harness off. She waits as he places it on a seat before squeezing onto two seats himself. She sits across from him beside the tanks. Still holding hands Multis and the sanguinarian sit beside each other a few seats in front of her.

Stärke leans towards her and asks in a whisper, "Has he seduced her?"

Achebe shakes her head. "Perhaps."

"That could be a problem," Stärke says.

But can Multis love or really have children she wonders.

As the tube starts moving she is surprised that the sanguinarian gets up and works his way to a seat across from her.

"What will you do when you meet the Perfect One?" the sanguinarian asks.

"We need to find someone," she answers honestly.

The sanguinarian squints suspiciously at her. "And what about the Maker's chosen people?"

She knows now that he is referring to his own people. "Find you another home."

"We like spaceships," he says with a tilt of his head so she can clearly see his fangs. "This one has partial gravity unlike those annoying pods."

She gulps. "You can keep this ship." His pale blue eyes and sensual voice are affecting her thinking.

"Good, that is what the Perfect One said. We will go with you wherever you must go but then we must have our freedom."

"Agreed," she replies than shakes her head. He's controlling the conversation.

They stop and a side glass door slides aside for them. The sanguinarian takes Multis's hand again and walks to an open elevator. He punches in a number on the keypad beside the elevator. The elevator is cylindrical and she can hear the exhale of air as the elevator is vacuumed upwards.

The door slides up and Achebe knows instantly they are in the control room. It's brighter in here and the sanguinarian hisses as he covers his face with one of his arms. "We will stay in the elevator," he says with a groan.

Achebe wonders at his meaning of the word *we.* "Is this what you want?" she asks Multis.

Multis winks at her and Achebe instantly knows she has only pretended to be under the sanguinarian's control.

Achebe hugs her before entering the control room.

Inside she sees a girl with rabbit ears and bare human feet covered in rabbit fur. She is holding a cross-bow aimed at the elevator.

She hears Stärke take in a deep breath as he gently puts his arm in front of her and walks into the room first. As he does she peers around for the one the sanguinarian called the Perfect One.

"Peace," she hears Stärke say to the lapine eared girl as he steps farther in.

There's a dull thud sound as she hears a familiar and deep voice full of terrible rage call out, "Thrain."

She steps forward and turns her head to the right. Stärke is up against the ship's wall with the King's hand around his throat.

"Let him go!" Achebe says as Multis enters the room. She hears a twang from the lapine girl's cross-bow.

Multis glances at the bolt in her side and scowling moves rapidly towards the lapine girl.

"Stop!" Achebe shouts trying to hold Multis back.

"Achebe?" the King asks.

"Yes," she says through gritted teeth as Multis drags her forward. She glances back and sees the lapine eared girl re-loading.

"Put your cross-bow down Abnoba," the King says as he drops Stärke to the floor.

"Don't hurt us Perfect One," the sanguinarian says from the shadows of the elevator.

Multis halts, the girl called Abnoba lowers her cross-bow, and Achebe bends over with her hands on her thighs gasping.

A perfectly shaped hand the colour of midnight reaches down to her. She holds onto it and feels the pounding of her heart calm.

The King turns to Stärke. "Who are you?" he asks with warning in his voice.

"Stärke," Achebe answers for him as she sees the giant man gasping for breath. "They used his genetics to make Thrain but they are only alike physically," she adds.

Achebe looks at the King's stomach where his belly should glow blue. She unbuttons his shirt and sees the scar where his belly button used to be. She thinks of her husband. "I can't go home yet, can I?" she asks looking up into the King's face.

"Soon," he tells her with a baritone voice that instantly soothes her. "We can meet up with your husband as we travel."

"To find the reliquia viviente?"

"And the Queen," he replies.

"And my sister Miya," the one called Abnoba adds.

She sees the distrustful squint of Multis's eyes. "You lied to me."

"Yes," Achebe replies. "Is the bolt deep?"

"Superficial. You would have died to protect the knowledge of this reliquia viviente?"

"Yes."

"Why?"

"Because we are all miniscule parts of something vast."

"And now what?" Multis asks as she gazes around the room.

"Will you come with me to put Bøddel into the pod we arrived on?"

Achebe doesn't miss the smirk that appears briefly on Multis's face. "You truly are wise Achebe." Multis picks up the welding harness and loops it around her shoulders.

Achebe turns to Stärke. "Stay with the King and...Abnoba...and rest," she says in a voice that is both gentle and authoritative.

"It will be interesting to observe when you and the Queen finally meet," the King says. She doesn't miss the amusement in his baritone voice.

CHAPTER NINE

"What is your name?" she asks the sanguinarian as he leads her and Multis back to Bøddel.

"Bram Rice," the sanguinarian replies. "I will expect something in return for all my help," he says to Multis.

"Oh, I'm sure you'll enjoy it," Multis replies with another wink at Achebe.

Bøddel is still standing near the door to the cafeteria he tore open. Achebe shudders at the sight. A golden headed deity of old with a silver body.

"Can we reprogram him?" she asks Multis.

Multis's entire body freezes and she stares lifelessly at Bøddel. Bram Rice lets go of her hand and steps back.

"What is she doing?" he asks.

Analysing I hope Achebe thinks to herself. *And not getting reprogrammed herself.* "I'm not sure," she replies honestly, "but we have to get to the pod we arrived on no matter what happens." If the pod overheats it will explode and tear a giant hole into the ship.

Multis's dead eyes become vibrant with life once again. Achebe watches as she strikes the top of Bøddel's head. Part of the golden sunray rises up with a casing. Inside the casing is a glowing red crystal. "Stay back!" Multis tells them.

As Achebe and the sanguinarian step away Achebe sees tiny strands of electrical bolts zap Multis's hands. The bolts suddenly cease and Multis hands are covered in streaks of black burn marks. A light keyboard appears out of the crystal.

Achebe cannot see any sign of pain in Multis's eyes but from the way her fingers move gingerly over the keys of the light keyboard she guesses Multis's is in great pain.

As Multis's replaces the crystal and bangs the top of the sunray back into place she says, "I will have to rest soon."

"What has happened to you my love?" Bram Rice asks with great concern in his voice.

"I knew there would be a safety mechanism," Multis's says in a slurred voice.

As Multis and Bram talk Achebe sees Bøddel walk towards the opposite door. "Can you make it to the control room?" she asks Multis.

"Yes," Multis replies with a slur.

In the control room, as the King inspects Multis's hands and while Bram Rice stays in the shadows of the elevator, Achebe watches the console's holographs.

She can see Bøddel enter the pod. It pushes buttons on the pod's console screen. She turns to another screen and sees the pod disconnect from the slavers' ship. The screen with Bøddel goes blank.

"We are leaving soon Achebe," the King tells her as he leans over the console and with a blur of his fingers programs the ship to depart the Thermosphere.

As her eyes stay glued to the holograph of the pod Bøddel is in she hardly notices the King strapping her in.

As the slavers' ship heads towards the exosphere she sees a red dot representing Bøddel leave a large yellow triangular symbol that represents the pod now on Sårad Värld.

A few moments later there is no more yellow symbol. Meanwhile, the red dot that represents Bøddel is moving in the direction she hoped it would. She slides the light map of Sårad Värld to where the Children of The Myth Machine is. "Do something worthy Bøddel," she whispers.

ACKNOWLEDGEMENTS

Gloria Antwi for modelling and confirming the meaning of the Adinkra symbols.

Kait McCord of for working with me to design the Adinkra symbol earrings and then creating them.

Kait can be reached at:

@34thandvinejewellerydesign

34thandvinejewellerydesign@gmail.com

Ethan Watt for the amazing star picture used for the front and back covers.

Andraya Watt for review the back cover.

Leah Weir for her insight.

Other books by Dan Watt (available through
Amazon Books as either e-book or paperback):

Queen of Caelum (the first book in the Children of
the Myth Machine series), fantasy/science fiction

Sylvia (the second book in the Children of the Myth
Machine series), fantasy/science fiction

Brackish (ship seven of the Future Wake series)
with Andy Watt, science fiction

Lucy & The Snivel Chair, mystery, science fiction

Dragon: The Emerald of Light, a medieval spoof

Dan Watt can be reached at:
mythruin@gmail.com

His websites are:

Caedar-writing-artwork.com

Mythruin.simplesite.com